War of Secrets

Kumar Nishant

Rajmangal Prakashan

An Imprint of **Rajmangal Publishers**

ISBN : 978-8119251131

Published by :

Rajmangal Publishers

Rajmangal Prakashan Building,
1st Street, Sangwan, Quarsi, Ramghat Road
Aligarh-202001, (UP) INDIA
Cont. No. +91- 7017993445
www.rajmangalpublishers.com
rajmangalpublishers@gmail.com
sampadak@rajmangalpublishers.in

प्रथम संस्करण : जून 2023 – पेपरबैक

प्रकाशक : राजमंगल प्रकाशन

राजमंगल प्रकाशन बिल्डिंग, 1st स्ट्रीट,

सांगवान, क्वार्सी, रामघाट रोड,

अलीगढ़, उप्र. – 202001, भारत

फ़ोन : +91 - 7017993445

First Published : June 2023 - Paperback

eBook by : Rajmangal ePublishers (Digital Publishing Division)

About the Author

"Kumar Nishant" is a marketing professional, born and brought up in the capital of Jharkhand, Ranchi.

Things change for sure, as one move forward with studies and is befriended by the responsibility. The only constant Kumar could survive, was his love for music which slowly led him into writing small pieces. What started with few slowly met the mirage of horizon.

A debutant with **"War of Secrets"**, Kumar is the winner of **"Foxclues India 100 Prime Authors Award – 2021"** for the same.

Preface

"War of Secrets" *was a story trapped in an imaginary space, occupied by the boundaries of amoebic confidence. It began as a clandestine operation, travelling in a cunning tunnel camouflaging as a daily routine.*

This book is dedicated to my dad, ***Late Surendra Kumar****, who was my first fan. He read this story in a single stretch when he first got it in his hand. Multiple times thereafter. The only qualification of mine for this honour was that I was his son. What more blessings can I ask for?* ***Miss you Papa****, and shall despise the vexatious corona till I die.*

Many believe that when Heavens bestow their blessings, Angels come down. For me it was my Mom, ***Mrs. Madhubala Surendra****. No matter how cagy I was, she could easily make out the different track of mine. Contrary to my expectation, the shy adventure was appreciated. In fact, she was happy that I was exploring a different dimension. She even walked an extra mile for me. As an ex professor of Hindi Literature, she rarely counted English writing in her friend list. However, she graced this one to superimpose it on the generally accepted theory of literary jargons defining any story, irrespective of the language chosen. It is here, the words lose their significance as a mode of expression.* ***Thank you mom for inspiring the "War of Secrets" to evolve on paper.***

Motherly prejudice may essentially loosen the effective checks. I had a force to counter it in the form of my sister, ***Shachi Priya****, who always had my back. I often wonder, how she shuffled being a painter by passion, an investment banker by choice and an avid reader for the rest of the time. Whatsoever, she readily agreed to deploy her creative instincts in conjunction with the varied reading* *experiences acquired by her. She played the role of my first critic to unleash the constructive reviews.* ***Gratitude though falling short for her help, is the only word for her****.*

When you are done with some hard work, it's the encouragement that counts. The universe didn't deprive me of it. Thanks to my brother **Kumar Mohit** *who was as happy as I was to see the story in a tangible form.*

I earnestly hope that "War of Secrets" is burnished to satisfaction as it emanates to a shape, aided by the pillars mentioned above.

Table of Contents

Chapter 1 - The Alert

"Good Morning Rajiv" – echoed a machine voice. Rajiv tried his best to ignore it, only to realize that the more he ignores it, the more intense it gets.

"Shut Up Alexa" – Shouted Rajiv as he opened his sleepy eyes while nagging about the early advent of morning.

He soon realized that tantrums are useless and he must be out of the bed to reach office on time. He sat cross-legged to sip his bed tea served by the robo butler – "Root".

"Chachu.. The story" – shouted Sneha in her sweet voice.

Sneha was Rajiv's niece who could not believe that there was a time without bots, Alexa, self-driving cars and other techs. She was enamored when Rajiv told her about his early days when these techs were a buzzword. Inquisitive as she was, she could not wait for Rajiv to settle down. She had followed the voice of Alexa and ran to Rajiv's room to hear more about life without gadgets and Internet of Things.

By the time Rajiv could smile and welcome her, she was already on his bed sitting in front of him. Rajiv quickly briefed her about his childhood and how he used to drive cars and bikes with manual transmission; his tete-a-tete at a coffee shop and commuting in an autorickshaw with a human driver. Sneha was stone-eyed and staring Rajiv as if trying to fathom Rajiv's story. To her, it seemed to be the gossip of the millennium.

"It's all real" - Rajiv asserted with a smile.

He promised Sneha to answer her questions in next sitting and requested her to leave so that he could get ready for office.

Sneha jumped off the bed, looked back and warned – " I'll be back Chachu". Rajiv nodded in agreement.

"Alexa – Please update on things to do today" was Rajiv's next command.

"Check your e-mails first. You haven't checked since yesterday night" – replied Alexa.

Rajiv unfolded his roll-top and looked deep into it to provide the retina scan for unlocking. He then transferred the screen content to the smooth finished walls of his room for reading e-mails while preparing for the office. Suddenly, there was an alarm with ⚠ sign all over the wall, in a red hue. The message was clear – "there's something grossly wrong in the office and Rajiv must rush". Rajiv had had such encrypted messages earlier, but not of the urgency as depicted in this one. He immediately doubled his speed and within no time was ready for his workplace.

"Saumya" – his wife, could read the tension by Rajiv's hurried actions. She quickly ordered "Alexa" to let the self-driving car on the portico.

"To office" – commanded Rajiv as he speedily entered the car. Even the machine could sense Rajiv's anxiety by now.

"Shall I further cool down the temperature" – asked "Rebecca", the digital personal assistant in Rajiv's car.

"No" – Said Rajiv deeply engrossed in his roll-top. Last week, though hectic, there was nothing serious at the workplace. Rajiv was trying really hard to guess what could have gone severely wrong.

On the other hand, even Saumya was worried. Rajiv had rushed to office in the past, and as a fallout had been away for a few days, but this time it was different. Rajiv was too tensed and didn't say goodbye to her before leaving. However, one thing she was sure – Rajiv won't be coming soon.

What was bothering her, was somehow or the other, she was bitten by an enigmatic premonition which was difficult to understand and express.

Chapter 2 - The Workplace Trouble

Rajiv got out of his car and ordered "Rebecca" to proceed to the parking area. He moved to his workstation and provided his retina scan to quickly boot up the system. There was a chit on the noticeboard, notifying a meeting in the conference hall in 5 minutes. Rajiv entered the conference hall to find "Sriram", his project lead with a network of systems projected on the wall.

Rajiv was part of a group of "Elite Geeks" who were involved in design and development of isolated modules of "Artificial Intelligence Defence Weaponry (AID-W)" which was a pilot program of the government. His team had completed module 1a and was working on phase 2 of the project.

"There has been a serious breach in our security protocol" – Began Sriram.

"Let me explain" - he said and slid the system nodes appearing on the wall.

The moment he pointed to a compromised node, there was a power cut with absolute blackout and the conference room was filled with smoke. Before Sriram, Rajiv or any other team member could figure out anything, they started to feel dizzy and passed out. They gained consciousness to find themselves across a beautiful dining table in an aesthetically designed dining hall, engulfing an enticing smorgasbord. They were surrounded by gunmen covered in masks and gears. It was obvious that they were in some kind of custody.

"Gentlemen, you must be tired. Please enjoy your meal and be refreshed. We are sorry for the trouble. Be rest assured, none of you will be harmed. We are talking with the government and soon you will be in your respective homes"

– echoed a human voice delivered through a high-end voice encryptor and modulator.

Everyone looked at one another in desperation to realize that there's no way out. The message was clear – they must not dare initiate any kind of conflicting action. Though suspicious, they reached out for the food. To everyone's surprise, the exotic delicacies lived up to their appearance and were exponentially complementary to the taste buds. The meal was sumptuous; but the question remained:

1. Why are they being treated with executive care?
2. What do these masked men want?
3. Are they enemy or friend?

However, pondering on such thought process was a futile exercise as they were not allowed to raise questions. Millions of queries were proliferating in each of the brains under custody, when they were hit by a loud chuck, turning on the television mounted on the wall of dining hall.

They could see themselves dining with a news flash - "***Tech team abducted from Government office***".

The hosts had recorded their lunch session and forwarded the clip to news agencies as a proof of life.

Reporting continued:

"The abductors have put forward their demands with an ultimatum of 20 days to the government to comply with. However, the Government is tight-lipped and reluctant to disclose the demands. So far, the only official statement from the Government is – "we are monitoring the situation and are in constant touch with the kidnappers. We shall do everything possible for the safe return of our personnel".

Hearing the coverage, Rajiv felt like being marinated with piquant for an archaic ritual of *"worshiping the prey before slaughter"*.

He wondered, how Saumya would be feeling. The answer was not far away. Saumya was on the television in a live telecast.

Conspicuously tensed and worried with saddened eyes, she appealed Government to ensure the release of her husband and his team at any cost.

"These 20 days are going to be 20 years for us. I request the kidnappers also to not use innocent people for their whatever fight. We are eagerly waiting for our family" – concluded Saumya.

Rajiv was thinking hard for the possible demands. What if the government did not agree? What if he is killed after 20 days deadline? Will he be subjected to atrocities?.

On the other side Saumya was also worried with similar questions. Will the government accede to demands? What after 20 days? Will Rajiv return?.

All these questions had a single answer – "No idea". The only chance Saumya and Rajiv had was to wait for the events to unfold, howsoever tough it might become.

Chapter 3 - Foe Or Friend

Convoluted within ifs and buts, Rajiv began to analyse the situation. To his surprise, being in a state of panic, he and other team members did not register that they were not robbed of their belongings. Their watches, wallets and most important of all, roll-tops and other communication devices were intact with them. He quickly tried to activate his watch which was connected to his home IOT network but in vain. Any signal trying to escape the walls were blocked in the facility where Rajiv and his team were contained.

Rajiv sat in pensive mood, trying to decipher whether the kidnappers were friendly or not.

He was suddenly shaken by a known voice – "Hello boys!!!".

Rajiv could make out that it was his office in charge, "Dr. Trinesh Shekhar Roy" – TSR as he was fondly known to everyone. The team in the room stood in disbelief as the sight of TSR became clearer.

"Welcome to a secret mission" - said TSR.

Everyone was keen to know the reason for which they were subjected to a series of petrifying events.

"Don't be dumbfounded. The circumstances were staged to help you work in seclusion and with utmost focus" – declared TSR.

The words, though simple, had more than enough potential to roll on the anxiety and add an extra momentum to blood pumping vessels of the heart of the entire team. TSR also informed that the families of the team were being constantly counselled and apprised about their well-being.

Dr. TSR seemed to have successfully eased out the chosen ones. However, he could easily identify the

perplexity on the faces. Apparently, common questions – why? What next?

Chapter 4 - The Secret

"Let's waste time no further and understand the problems. Please follow me to the discussion room" – requested Dr. TSR.

Soon everybody was in a well-furnished conference hall with the translucent and projectable walls on the front and back side.

"We have been working on a highly confidential and ambitious project of the government to make us future ready" – Began Dr. TSR.

Let me give you a quick recap of our project:

Phase 1:

- *Creation of robots capable of penetrating the enemy lines.*

- *Compacting the size and giving them the ability to record and transmit information*

- *Fitting weapon system and controlled Artificial Intelligence (AI).*

Phase 2:

- *Instill the ability in robots to communicate with each other through controlled AI*

- *Program them to understand the various schemes of co-ordinated weapon deployment system in view of the possibility of different kinds of weapons that can be attached to different bots.*

- *Enhance their capability to form a well-disciplined army of robots who can dynamically deploy themselves in the best suited formation and co-ordinated weapon scheme. Thus, they can have the ability to launch an all-out offensive.*

"Gentlemen, we are making ourselves future ready. The wars and invasions shall no longer be dominated by the humans. It's going to be technology that can make or break a nation. We have successfully completed the β version of Phase 1 and are parallelly pursuing Phase 2" – revealed Dr. TSR.

Rajiv and the entire team felt a thrilling shockwave through their spines. They were never aware that their assignment was a part of highly confidential X-File.

"Sir, what are we supposed to do now ??" – asked Rajiv enthusiastically.

"There's a problem" – said Dr. TSR in a very serious tone.

We have a special facility built for our project. Security breach discovered by "Sriram" is not the only one. We have also discovered unauthorized access attempt in the logs of our special facility access. That too, when it has not been disclosed to the outside world. We suspect it to be from trans-national boundary. Also, the trojans were found in some systems. We don't know how many nodes have been bugged. We needed additional support to contain the intrusion and prevent the project from being stolen.

The geek within Rajiv could not wait to get into action. He was imagining what the special facility would look like and will he be really able to counter the unknown but seemingly skilled enemy.

"Am I capable enough? What will he/they be like?" – thought Rajiv.

Chapter 5 - Finding The Enemy

"We shall be leaving around 04:00 hrs in the morning to our confidential facility. Till then, have rest; because after that you might not be able to. Remember, the government has only 20 days. We ought to finish our job in time. It's Hobson's choice" – informed TSR.

Anxiety did not allow Rajiv to sleep. By the time, the feeling sank, it was already 04:00 hrs. Rajiv decided to have a nap during the journey. He didn't even know when he slept. He was wakened up by TSR at the gate of the facility for security check.

It was nothing like what Rajiv had imagined. He was thinking of a secret passage through a Royal headquarter like building, with all modern amenities and guarded by handsomely dressed security personnel.

On the contrary, Rajiv found himself somewhere in the middle of a desert, maybe in Rajasthan, where an undecorated, prison like impermeable gate camouflaged to mix with the surrounding, welcomed the visitors. But the moment they were in and descended to a mezzanine floor, Rajiv's imagination came to life. It was a heavily guarded facility with all the amenities.

"This facility is not traceable even by the satellites. The only entry to this desert facility, is through a secret passage which opened up right in front of the gate they saw at security check post" – explained Dr. TSR.

Rajiv was awestruck by the systems installed in the facility. They were all "**HT-GTAX-IV**" which had only been mentioned in some magazines and had a few leaked details exclusively on the dark web. Enthralled by the beauty of machines, barely did Rajiv notice that Dr. TSR was smiling from a corner who was well aware of Rajiv's passion towards machines.

"Like it??" – Said Dr. TSR with a chuckle.

Embarrassed as he was, Rajiv replied in affirmation with kid's shyness and asked – "When do we start ??".

"Let me show you the network structure in the discussion room. In the meantime your authentication cards are being prepared so that you all can have full access to the machines" - Dr. TSR had already projected 3D model of the installed network on the walls.

He quickly briefed about the LAN arrangements and also provided a walk-through of the facility.

"Let's go for a real tour now and meet the facility experts to understand their findings" – invited TSR after the virtual tour.

The group over there was headed by Mr. Arya Sheshan, who pleasantly greeted Sriram and his team. He showed them the screenshot of the log underlining the multiple attempts of unauthorized access and expounded :

"After few minutes, the unauthorized entries were automatically deleted. We tried to trace the location of the attack, but could not, as the log data showed multiple locations in each attempt. We also found trojans (a malicious program) in various systems. As a precautionary measure, we immediately went offline and are presently scanning other machines in the setup, to find out the number of affected nodes. The matter is of great concern, as the spectrum, we are operating in is not open to service providers and commercial applications. It seems to be a well-planned conspiracy by a real skilled adversary to lay hands on our project"

"Sir, virus is everywhere. We surmise, that the spread is phenomenal" – words of the admin was a calling for Sheshan.

"Quite a number of machines are yet to be scanned. I shall join you in some time. Till then, you are free to understand the network and mull over possible solutions" – Sheshan said as he left.

"Can you recognize the machines installed over here" – Sriram asked the team, as Sheshan proceeded for his work.

Members reacted in negative except Rajiv, who almost spontaneously replied – "**HT-GTAX-IV**".

Sriram looked at Rajiv in astonishment and said – "Wonderful, at least now we know the system. Any plans Rajiv? Since you are the one who can identify the configuration and machine, I think you must take the lead. Team members and I shall support".

Rajiv readily agreed. "Let's try to recover the log" – he said.

"Wouldn't they have already tried" – snubbed Sriram.

"I am not talking about the logs auto stored at application level. We must access the root. There is an inbuilt security provision in "HT-GTAX-IV". But it can only be obtained through the manufacturer's key which should have been provided during the procurement and installation of network. If not, we must contact the suppliers. Let the government get it for us" – Rajiv explained.

"No, unfortunately we don't have them over here. These are military grade equipment manufactured in Europe and contacting suppliers to seek such sensitive information requires to flow through a set of procedures. We don't have time. I don't think we can wait for the government procedures" – came the reply along with Sheshan, who was back; just in time, to hear Rajiv's statement of getting manufacturer's keys.

"Can you get into the system without manufacturer's keys? We don't have much of a choice." – added Sheshan.

"Well, in that case, do you have administrator access to the boot level of the server" – asked Rajiv. To Rajiv's delight, Sehshan's reply was positive. Rajiv tried really hard and was successful in controlling his anxiety and a stupendous stimulus that could have led to an ostensible outburst of his dark side.

Rajiv had been a notorious hacker in the past and was well versed with the dark web associated with hacking activities. The good thing was that he never supported or indulged in using the knowledge to harm remote data or for malpractices like creation of ransomware or other detrimental and illegal programs. He just derived thrill from defying the claims that a highly secured full proof system has been built that is beyond any techies ability to break through.

Enamoured by the in principle permission to break through one of the world's most secure systems, Rajiv could feel the benign tremor emanating from the sudden jostling force of rising adrenaline junky within his soul.

Sheshan then asked – "Will the administrative access suffice?".

"May be. But do initiate the process of getting the manufacturer's keys. Just for worst case, if at all it comes to it" – said Rajiv.

"We have only 18 days now" – Sheshan turned to Sriram.

"Don't worry, we will do our level best" – said Sriram.

"I have faith in you Rajiv. What do you think? How long will it take to get to the root" – asked Sriram.

"Can't say. This monster is less known. Let's see what's inside. I am sure this server must be having quite a robust security system" – replied Rajiv.

"Ok then. You play with your server and in the meantime, let me and other team members check the damage done by the trojans. And yes, do reach out for us in case any help is required" – uttered Sriram as he moved away with other team members to check the nodes.

Rajiv smiled and started working on the trespassed "HT-GTAX-IV-S" server. He was thinking that it should be really easy as he is having the administrative permission to enter the system. Little did he know that he was in for a surprise.

To his astonishment, the encryption within the server was really advanced. He could not break through them using the so called "Special algorithms" which he had earlier deployed to gain access to highly acclaimed secure systems. For next 15 hours he was sitting with his roll-top connected to the server and trying various permutation & combination of skills & programs which were privy to hackers on the dark web and till date not readily accessible to general academics. All, leading to a dead end.

Exasperated by the constant rebuke of the machine, Rajiv felt like crushing it into fine pieces. Just then, adding on to the ire came a question piercing Rajiv's ear "Any luck Rajiv" – it was Sriram inquiring as he took a break from scanning of various nodes.

"Negative !!!" – Replied Rajiv in frustration while thinking "Goddamn!!! there could have been a better moment for this??".

"Come on.. you are the best and we cannot give up. Let's have a break. You have been engrossed like hell" – pepped Sriram as he moved towards the coffee machine.

Rajiv smiled and accompanied him. They were soon joined by Sheshan who informed that they are in the process of getting the manufacturer's key for the worst case. But considering the contractual and legal formalities involved on both sides, it doesn't seem to happen anywhere before 12-15 days.

"The problem then will be that even with the optimistic estimate of 12 days, we will be left with only 4-5 days to meet the deadline of 20 days. Seeking any extension will be difficult as it may create both civil and political restlessness in the outside world" – Remarked Sheshan.

"I have full faith in Rajiv. Let's be patient for at least one more day" – Asserted Sriram.

But Rajiv's mind was elsewhere. He seemed to be registering only half of the conversation going on. Sole good thing he could comprehend was that he had one more day while simultaneously feeling the brunt of faith posed in him by Sriram.

Sheshan could make out Rajiv's disconnect from the conversation and asked him to take some rest. "Rajiv, you have been working continuously since 15 hours. It is now reflecting in your eyes. We can't afford to be sick. Go, get some sleep. We can talk tomorrow evening on the progress" – he elaborated with an intension to dilute the noticeable pressure felt by Rajiv.

Though reluctant, Rajiv agreed. Deep within, even he was convinced that a fresh approach might be needed to pass through the encryption. After all, he was at loggerheads with one of the most secure systems in the world.

Rajiv could not sleep for long. He was awake within a span of few hours. He was quick to grab on a cup of coffee after a rapid freshening up. He began to ponder upon the possible bottleneck in his approach.

It was clear that encryption was an advanced version of "Secure Hashing Algorithm (SHA)" coupled with time consideration.

Suddenly, something struck into his mind. Rajiv's program always used to time out. He did not get any error message with respect to his commands. If that was the case, maybe, the computing power of his roll-top was not enough to meet the requirements. He needed to find a way to increase the computing speed. Possibly, he could use another "HT-GTAX-IV" and overclock it to enhance the processing speed.

Having figured out a probable approach, he rushed to configure another system to interact with the special access server. It took almost half of the day to set up the system. Rajiv knew he was running against time, but the plan seemed logical and he decided to take a chance. Though, the program initiated without hiccups, results could not be guaranteed as of yet.

Rajiv was sipping his coffee in nervousness. He knew it might happen in a few minutes or it may take hours. He was left with no option but to test his luck. Nevertheless, he was in no mood to leave any stone unturned. While he let the system do its work, Rajiv started checking his roll-top for other tools in his quiver. Just in case, the logic he just bet on goes awry. He kept his fingers crossed and was hoping desperately that he is able to pass on a good news to Sheshan in the evening.

"Whatever!!!" – said Rajiv to himself after exploring his roll-top for some time on the course of his march towards the dining table.

Rajiv finished his lunch and immediately reached out for his roll-top to chalk out plan "B" to be triggered, if the ongoing attempt failed. He worked for an hour or two and decided to have a little rest before checking out the setup he did in the first half. However, rest, relaxation or any other such synonyms seemed to be on the other side of the spectrum for Rajiv. At the very instance, Rajiv heard a pleasant beeping cacophony originating from the computing machine which sounded like an elite opera performance to his ears. All his basking intentions withered away and he rushed to the 2 “HT-GTAX-IV” he had set up.

He saw the screen and yelled at the top of his voice – “Yes, I Did it”.

The brief broadcast was enough to give goose bumps to anybody falling within its periphery.

“Yes, that’s my boy!!” – Sriram punched the air while rushing towards Rajiv.

He was speculating about the possible findings of Rajiv. “Has he been able to trace the enemy? Would it be easy for him to handle the cyber intrusion??” and many more such questions were revolving in his brain.

There was only one answer to it – “Rajiv and his discovery”. However, it was unknown to him as yet.

Chapter 6 - Finding Location

Soon everybody gathered around Rajiv. Curious like a kid, they waited for him to elucidate the decrypted message.

"Shall I call Sheshan?" – asked Sriram to which Rajiv nodded in affirmation.

Sheshan was there in minutes, gasping for his breath. It was evident that he almost ran to reach the spot.

"Show me, what you people have got" – he said impatiently.

Rajiv then started:

"We have got access to the root and could detect at least 5 attempts on the server. It is the sheer computing prowess of HT-GTAX-IV that stored the data before it was erased at the application level. If we can somehow extract the metadata and are able to track the IP addresses stored therein, we may be able to identify the coordinates of location which triggered the intrusion".

"Well done Rajiv. You have saved more than a few precious days for us. How long will it take to decipher the location?" – applauded Sheshan with a simultaneous discharge of question.

"I am sure, the IPs are dynamically generated to camouflage the real location. Time frame depends on the hopping mechanism followed by the attackers" – answered Rajiv.

"I can't wait to get to them. Let's make it quick. If you have passed through the military grade system, I believe you can trace this too" – confidence was palpable in Sheshan's voice as he said this to Rajiv.

"Let me analyze and then we can say something" – Rajiv reciprocated with equal confidence.

He then downloaded the data from the root log and started dissecting the addresses. As truly guessed by the hacker residing in his soul, the addresses were dynamically generated to hide their original location. Rajiv could make out that his counterpart was ain't novice or a cakewalk to deal with. Even the HT-GTAX-IV could not record the complete address log. The unknown was quick to deploy the malware and out of the system in no time.

Rajiv figured out that in all the 5 attempts, identical no. of hopping were recorded. He had to spend more than a few hours to find the co-ordinates of all the addresses he could gather. In the winning jiffy of an ephemeral cyber battle, Rajiv forgot that he had been working continuously on the machines without any break. Eye-opener came in the form of pinching pain in his back and neck. Realising it to be the wee hours, Rajiv decided to call it a day and carry on with the analysis next morning. Rajiv went to bed with some respite, boosted confidence and resolve to take on the hacker to the best of his ability.

He was up before dawn, seemingly controlled by enormous energy coxed to his subconscious mind.

"Battle is won, but the war is on" – said Rajiv to himself, as if, having attained Nirvana with a prodigious morning wisdom.

He was greeted by Sriram and Sheshan on the breakfast table. They informed that purging of trojans from nodes was almost done.

"We feel the trojans were disseminated from the nodes connected to restricted outside world and found their way into the server" – added Sriram.

"Even I feel the same. But a different malware was also uploaded in the server." – acknowledged Rajiv.

His subconscious mind was quick to recall the root log he cracked few hours ago which confirmed the uploading of malware.

"What's the story at your end?" – asked Sheshan.

"I could figure out about 5 unauthorized attempts at nodes. I am trying to decode the hopping algorithm and zero in on the possible location of the enemy. Let's see who are we dealing with. I think by lunch we can have some more idea. Once we are done with the nodes, we will dissect the server malware and its intentions" – briefed Rajiv.

"Ok then. We move to finish with the remaining nodes and you take care of the coordinates. We'll meet at lunch with some progress… hopefully!!" – said Sriram with a smile.

Rajiv quickly hooked on to his roll-top and began to pinpoint the locations described by the co-ordinates he collected last night. The enemy was shrewd enough to make the addresses scatter around the globe, rendering guesswork a sort of arcane witchcraft. Everything was a heavily jumbled puzzle, with no solution.

Rajiv looked at the data with a cunning smile. He seemed to be possessed by a latent conviction of having the ability to break through with the snap of a finger.

He arranged the addresses in 5 sets corresponding to each attempt he could trace. He translated the location co-ordinates into titles known to the world. He believed that some pattern would emerge and he can easily decode the attacker's location. However, things were easier said than done. Even after considering all the 5 sets together, no single location was repeated.

An hour passed and Rajiv was at an impasse with a kind of messed up brain teaser. He was fidgeting with anything falling within proximity. With his latent overconfidence blown into pieces, he was clearly feeling the brunt of being an impregnable bulwark.

Scared by the possible failure, Rajiv invoked the self-consolation mode and said to himself:

"There must be something behind the obvious. I must renunciate haste in favour of sanity. It's time for cautious scrutiny and reinventing the wheel".

He calmly looked at the dataset and started afresh. After diligent analysis of each set in isolation, Rajiv decided to cross examine them by juxtaposing against each other. He could figure out a specific entity in each of them – **"Location in Africa".** Though not repeating but they were surprisingly close to each other.

Rajiv noticed that it was 10 minutes to lunch and thought of lying down to relax a bit. Soon he was under the influence of an uncontrollable short nap. By the time he got up, he was a little late for luncheon. He hurried to the dining table, only to find Sheshan and Sriram discussing over a scoop of dessert.

"Sorry, I just had an unintentional nap" – Said Rajiv while picking up his plate.

"Don't be, we saw you and decided that you do need it" – whispered Sriram.

"Could you make out something?" – Spoke Sheshan with hopeful eyes.

"I can only guess that it's some place in Africa. We need to build a trap" – said Rajiv.

Chapter 7 - The Trap

"Trap" – frowned Sheshan.

"Could you elaborate" – asked Sriram.

Rajiv explained:

"I intend to build a ***blockchain*** *resting behind a frontend, which simulates a security level required to be broken into, to gain access to any confidential info. We then send signal to hackers that we are* ***'up and working'****. In reality, they need to mine and add a node to our blockchain to complete the process. We will be prepared and waiting for the attack. As soon as it happens, we can deliberately tweak the mining difficulty, if required, and prevent the process from completing until our systems trace and record the hacker's origin. They can then delete the application log and leave"*

"I believe, we can then pinpoint the location co-ordinates" – concluded Rajiv.

"Will the plan work?? How long will it take to build and test the trap??" – Intervened Sheshan.

"I 'am hopeful. In fact, it should work. I think we can build the application in 4-5 days. But we will need the support of the entire team out here" – said Rajiv with a grin.

"Ok. Then we all meet within half an hour" – concluded Sriram.

About half an hour later, everybody assembled in the hall and Rajiv explained his idea to them. Sheshan and Sriram were carefully observing the reaction of the gathering. Obviously, they were a little sceptical of the idea and worried about the loss of time; in case, it bombed on their face. But the smallest of their doubt was blown away, when technical experts present in the room supported it unanimously.

"Let's attempt to finish the trap as early as possible and meet in 5 days" – said Sheshan while leaving with Sriram in his chamber.

The others carried on with the strategy. It was finally decided that the program shall be developed in 4 modules. Accordingly, the entire team was divided into 4 groups with dedicated responsibilities.

Group 1: design of front end user interface.

Group 2: simulation of security features.

Group 3: development of dummy database giving the impression of confidential data.

Group 4: design of Blockchain.

"Let's finish the conceptualization of modules by today. We can then finalize the integrated architecture by lunch tomorrow" – proposed Rajiv.

After getting nod from everyone, he moved out of the hall to work on the "Blockchain" module. He finished his job by evening. But there were multiple thoughts in his mind. The biggest challenge faced by the seemingly uncomplicated program, was to perfectly validate the pretence as reality.

Rajiv knew that the enemy was equally competent. Any slight mistake may lead to the discovery of the trap. Keeping it in mind, he started preparing a checklist for monitoring salient parameters while finalizing the integrated architecture. While in the middle, something struck his mind and he hurried towards Sheshan's chamber.

"Hi" – greeted Rajiv

"Oh yes. Is everything ok?" – replied Sheshan in a perplexed mode. He was definitely not expecting him.

"Nothing serious. We're on track. I was wondering, in case you have spare machines, we can use them for development purpose. Actually, as a precautionary measure, I don't want to use the systems which are in use and are active in the existing network" – disclosed Rajiv.

Sheshan immediately eased out. His worries were befittingly addressed. He passed on a wizardly smile with a touch of narcissism.

"Follow me" – he commanded Rajiv.

Sheshan was walking as if he was an emperor about to unveil his hidden treasure. Indeed, what he revealed was no less than that. He led Rajiv to a hall hosting a series of **"HT-GTAX-IV"** – all ready to join the network.

"We always keep spare machines. You never know what may come up and resources may be required in a short span. Like now" – said Sheshan

"Goodness me !!!" – came the words from Rajiv's mouth and his stunned eyes were wide open in amazement.

"I'll ensure that these are allocated to you and the rest of the team. Anything else ??" – asked Sheshan.

"No" – replied Rajiv.

The sheer sight of new systems invigorated new energy in Rajiv. He quickly finished his checklist and prepared for the next day's meeting.

As planned, Rajiv and team finalized the conceptualization by lunch. Sheshan was not behind either. He kept his promise and before everybody finished their meal, the pristine systems were in place for their work.

Every member went on their toes and the software was ready in 4 days – a day ahead of schedule. Rajiv proudly informed the feat to Sheshan.

"What next ??" – asked Sheshan.

"We've completed testing. It's time for deployment" – said Rajiv.

"How ??" – Sriram joined the conversation.

"The plan is simple. Let's revisit the network and select the most appropriate decoy" – answered Rajiv.

He then requested Sheshan to explain the digital facility once again. As Rajiv analytically examined Sheshan's words, he finally landed in astonishment.

"How could I miss it !!!" – exclaimed Rajiv.

"I don't understand" – frowned Sheshan.

Rajiv elucidated:

"The entire network is essentially offline. The exception is only one stand alone system connected to extranet with the sole purpose of communication of the encrypted status message or meeting requests. Now that's the only system hackers can target and get into. But the malware was also found in the offline setup. That's difficult to explain".

"Oops!!. Even we overlooked it. Now, that's the start of a new puzzle. Seems we are back to square one" – cribbed Sheshan in anguish.

Chapter 8 – So Near So Far

"Save your energy. We will need it. Can't you see; at least we are done with the purging of malware. Everything is not that gloomy sheshan" – Sriram tried to control the nerves.

Sheshan nodded while still in pensive mood. He then looked at Rajiv, who caught the subtle message and moved towards the only machine connected to the internet for a brief explanation:

"This is the only entry point for any infiltration attempt. I am sure, the enemy must have put this node under surveillance. Having done that, I believe, they will definitely try to access it once we go online. If this is the case, we must create a clone of this system to ensure backup and eliminate any risk of data loss. And that's precisely what we'll stick to. Next, we deploy our program in the system and go online. That's it!!!. We then finally wait for our prey"

"What if they don't come" – Sheshan raised the doubt.

"Well, in that case, we are out of luck. But I am sure, they will" – there was an inexplicable confidence in Rajiv's voice.

It was actually the hacker within. But Rajiv knew, he must not reveal his dark side at any cost.

"How long will you wait" – Sriram reminded of the deadline.

"Max, for a day. If not successful, then we shall explore the other options" – said Rajiv.

"Do you have one ??" – asked Sheshan soaked in quandary.

"Actually, not yet. But I mean, we will have to" – even Rajiv appeared shaky this time.

"Let's work on this one first. Who knows, we might not need an alternate plan. It's like pronouncing judgement before the crime" – Sriram stepped in again to counter the negativity.

"Hmm…. How long Rajiv ??" – Sheshan shot a kind of encrypted question.

"We can be live by tomorrow morning" – replied Rajiv

"Ok. Then see you tomorrow. I'll have a break" – Sheshan moved out of the room with the declaration.

Rajiv didn't waste another second and initiated the cloning procedure on the earmarked system. He and others, finished the deployment at around midnight and set the system online with immediate effect. Next step was announcement to the outside world.

Rajiv did not want to take any chance. He called up Sheshan for help in the transmission of an authenticated message. Sheshan obliged and was there within 5 minutes. He logged in and forwarded a harmless message with proper authentication and encryption.

"What was this for ??" – he turned towards Rajiv.

"A true lie for the enemy. They must know that we are back on our highly confidential assignment. The moment they try to enter, an alarm will be triggered." – Rajiv confirmed the ploy.

"Now, we wait for the enemy's move, right !!" – Said Sheshan.

"Can I join you all" – he requested further.

Unpretentious request of Sheshan won everyone's heart. Together, they waited with finger's crossed, hoping for the sound of alarm. They had a lot of discussion, both related and unrelated to the task. It all happened till 4:30 in the morning.

"Even rest is important. Let's have some. Alarm is always there to wake us up" – ordered Sheshan to everyone comprehending the tired faces around him.

While the others fell asleep, Rajiv pondered upon the worst case scenario : ***"What if they don't attack ??".***

He had no answer to that. But the question had a cruel effect on his sleeping pattern. The "on" and "off" oscillation was considerably frequent. Alarm blew up at around 7:15 a.m., piercing through the heartbeat of sleeping bodies with domineering impact on Rajiv. He was up and behind the "HT-GTAX-IV" in no time, as if, a radicalized programmer.

Deeply engrossed in tweaking the security requirements to ensure the tracing of enemy address, little did Rajiv notice, that in the process, he was joined by all the other members including Sheshan and Sriram. His digital arrest was permeated by a loud co-ordinated clapping; the moment monitor depicted a successful tracing.

Rajiv felt like winning the battle and quickly shifted to getting the co-ordinates. To his dismay, he was still unable to pin-point the location. The best he could figure out was that the attacker was somewhere near **Mali, Africa.**

Rajiv shared his finding with a restrained enthusiasm. He noticed a strange reaction from Sheshan. He was trying extremely hard to recall something.

"We all are up since long. Let's call it a day and allow for recuperation of gray matter. We can bang our heads from tomorrow" – said Sheshan and went up to his chamber.

He secretly advised Rajiv to meet him in his chamber after a few minutes as he left.

"I saw you noticed me and are curious. But I cannot disclose anything yet. I believe, we can get something for you tomorrow. But till then no discussion on this with anyone;

not even Sriram" – instructed Sheshan as Rajiv entered his chamber.

Rajiv couldn't understand a thing. But Sheshan's alarmingly tensed voice made him commit to comply without any questions.

Chapter 9 – The Traitor

Next morning, Sheshan congratulated everyone for tracing the location to Mali. He then continued:

*"Rajiv's utterance of Mali struck a chord in my mind. It took me a while, but I could recall the tech support – **"Shah",** who used to emphatically tell stories about Mali, the neighbouring Timbuktu and presence of Taliban in the area. We nabbed him on suspicion. Following his revelations, we surmise the involvement of Italian Mafia in stealing our weapon system and use it for earning super normal profits in the illegal weapon market. Shah met one of the **"mafia agents"** during an official meeting convened to finalize a deal for high end systems with an Italian firm. Fond of bragging as he was, he showcased himself being a part of a special team serving at some extremely secured location. He was then tracked and contacted by the agent and lured into sharing the IP details of only connected system of this facility.*

But the most important question remained. It was a standalone system. How did the malware reach the server and other nodes. That's because no external device is allowed or used in this facility. Things became interesting from here. Shah, on the pretext of maintenance, connected the server to this standalone system. He then downloaded the malware transferred by the enemy. All this was perfectly planned and executed. The timing of attack coincided with the maintenance activity. This was crucial as Shah cannot log in and forward any authorized message from the system, thereby broadcasting a clue. So the plan was based on a synchronized-watch model. Shah accessed the server on a pre agreed time, transferred the malware and easily walked out as he was not in possession of any external device. Things went haywire, when they tried to get in multiple times after securing the details from Shah and was caught by our team. Nevertheless, it was good for us. It was this greed that led us to Mali"

"Rajiv, can you hack the system of enemy and destroy them" – asked Sheshan.

"I can infiltrate and corrupt any system or network, provided I am in and connected to it. But, in case the data are residing somewhere else which is not connected to the ecosystem, I am helpless" – Responded Rajiv with a caveat.

"As of now, I think, we need to ascertain 2 information. First, how much of the data has been given. Second, has the data been distributed. Well, that's my job. You all may have another day off. See you all tomorrow !!" – Sehshan bid adieu while reaching out for the hotline connection.

He was gone, leaving everyone waiting impatiently for a new sunrise. Following morning, Sheshan was welcomed by a strong inquisitive vibe as he entered the conference hall where everyone had gathered to listen to him. Without much ado, sheshan began the briefing :

"It is indeed them – the Italian Mafia. Cogitating Shah's description, we created a sketch of the agent who lured him. We could successfully identify him through the records available with intelligence agencies and corroborated by the Interpol.

During interrogation, shah regurgitated the entire deal. He was brainwashed and promised an unbelievable and hefty kickback, both in cash and kind. He was to receive 50% on the infiltration of system and 50% on handing over the sensitive information. Shah had not yet received the other 50%. In fact, he was due to meet the mafia in next 15 days. The agenda being, how to sneak a cloning device into the server. This means, the enemy does not have enough data.

That may be considered as a good news. But we don't want any risk on account of accidental ignorance. We are investigating from various angles and waiting for a little more information and inputs from other government agencies".

By the time, Sheshan was done sharing the info, he could visibly notice the unwinding effect on the face of each and every official present in the room. It had been tough for them with enough of setbacks and series of alternate plans. Now, they were looking forward to an enjoyable lunch.

Post lunch, Sheshan was constantly on his phone. The expressions on his face transformed like a travelling sine wave, covering all the possible shades of astonishment. It was followed by a few fax messages. He carefully examined them and rang up Rajiv.

"We both missed something" – a single sentence was enough to pull Rajiv in Sheshan's chamber.

"You remember, there was a cyber attack in your office too" – reminded Sheshan while ordering coffee for two.

"Yes. Is it linked too ??" – Rajiv was taken by surprise.

"Of course, it is. The common link is the mafia. They have been trying to tap anything that they can. The game is big. If not the entire weaponry, they can sell the prototype at government level" – described Sheshan.

"I still don't get that. Even we didn't know what we were working on. The project simply had a confidential tag, but like many other assignments. How did these people get to know about it ??. It's unrelatable that an International Mafia will go after a very ordinary government office" – Rajiv just couldn't put the pieces together.

"We forwarded sketch of the agent to our security agencies for any available information. He was spotted with

Shah near your office, a day before the cyber attack" – explained Sheshan.

"But I never knew anyone named Shah in my office??" – countered Rajiv.

Sheshan felt Rajiv's state of confusion and decided to divulge the other side of the story.

"There are rumours on the backstage of International community, that we are working on some very hi-tech, never seen before weaponry. That too, when there's no official communication about it. Thanks to some sections of our over-enthusiastic media. The unverified news drew attention of many, including the topmost and prominent illegal organizations. Every, confidential project of government came on their radar. That's how they reached your office. Shah is not the culprit as far as your office is concerned. He just met the agent at a place chosen by him. But fortunately, for us it highlighted the node we did not look much into".

Sheshan's explanation caught up to the nerves of Rajiv.

"What did they get from my office ?? Before Sriram could brief us, we were all into your plan and absolutely forgot about it" – he asked.

"I have already discussed with Sriram. The system they hacked had some theoretical information about the program. By God's grace, they were out of luck. Sriram was in the office who intercepted them quickly and disconnected the entire office network. Hackers couldn't stay in for long. But we don't know how much they have stolen" – replied Sheshan.

"I know about the theoretical information you are talking about. We came out with it for ease of prototype development of modules we were working on" – informed Rajiv.

"There are grey areas and we can't take chances. We are working on a plan. Be ready to rise up for the occasion. You might have to play an important role in our plan. Have a good rest. Will let you know the details by evening" – concluded Sheshan with an impish smile.

"OK", replied Rajiv with simultaneous murmuring - "You want me to rest after pulling me into an unknown plan !!".

"Did you say something" – asked Sheshan.

"Nothing" – said Rajiv while thinking frantically – "What am I gonna get into next ??"

Chapter 10 – The Journey

Sheshan called Rajiv after dinner and told him about the plan:

"We don't know what data is in the possession of the enemy and how may offices they are tracking. Under the circumstances, we have no option but to track and hunt down their set up. The good news is we have found the exact location of the base of the Italian mafia. The enemy is in the heart of ***Timbuktu,*** *a part of* ***The Republic of Mali.*** *You see, technology, howsoever advanced, has its own limitations. Sometimes, rudimentary manual approach is a must to achieve the goal. We have contacted the Mali Government and they have agreed to help in containing them. You will be leaving to Mali as a part of a secret defense delegation with a camouflage of bilateral trade meet. You will team up with our field officer* ***"Aryan",*** *and if required, you both will enter the hostile facility and destroy the network over there."*

"What !!!" – exclaimed Rajiv with exasperation.

"Don't worry, you won't be alone. Aryan will be there for you. Prepare yourself; he will be here by morning and all your official documents will also be ready by then. We shall leave after the breakfast. Remember, you will have maximum 4 days in Mali. In case you fail, we will go all offensive with the help of Mali government in destroying the mafia base" – Sheshan tried to pacify and boost Rajiv.

Rajiv understood that he had no say. It's a kind of order wrapped in conversation. The plan has already been decided and finalized. He agreed to Sheshan with his own set of doubts, excitement and fear.

Earlier, in the course of tracking the hackers, Rajiv often yearned to see the enemy set up that created havoc in one of the most secure facility equipped with the latest systems, not even heard by many.

"But I never wanted it at the peril of my life" – thought Rajiv.

That night Rajiv, assembled all the tools and gadgets he thought he might require for the task.

He met Aryan at the breakfast table.

Aryan was a very handsome face attached to a strongly built and perfectly chiselled physique. His every movement exuberated the likes of a highly trained, war mongering soldier, passionate about accomplishment of any mission, whatsoever.

"What if he was inside the enemy lines and Aryan expected him to aid his manoeuvres" – imagined Rajiv.

"Oh God. Man, I am a techie…!!, no soldier !!" – thoughts abruptly broke the boundaries of brain and rode on the boisterous vocal cord of Rajiv.

"Don't worry, you won't die. It's also a part of my mission to keep you alive" – it was the husky voice of Aryan.

"If we are in, then we are !! No further thoughts. Let me get my paraphernalia" – said Rajiv.

By 10:00 am Sheshan, Rajiv and Aryan took off from New Delhi airport, en route to Mali along with other delegates. Sitting next to Aryan, Rajiv was on a wilful transcend to immerse himself in the excitement of digital adventure held by the future. But it was all in vain. He was overpowered by the butterflies of fear jumping in his stomach.

"What's the plan" – asked Rajiv.

"As of now, nothing. Will make one, once we reach Timbuktu" – Aryan replied with utmost calm, but it aggravated Rajiv's latent chill, ready to run through his spine.

Aryan's response was an instant burial of Rajiv's attempt to fathom the unknown menace. He then turned to Sheshan in hope of resurrection. This time, the fate was against him. Sheshan was enjoying a peaceful nap.

"I don't even know, if I will be a part of the return journey, and these guys seem to be on a pleasure trip. It may be normal for them, not me, damn it !!" – thought Rajiv.

He was in no mood to give up and waited for Sheshan to come around. He posed the same question to him and received a reply identical to that of Aryan's. During the next 21 hours of journey, Rajiv made multiple attempts, covered in a variety of questions to extract the plan. But all of them ended in a black hole, as Sheshan and Aryan didn't take much time to comprehend Rajiv's fear psychosis of head on collision with the enemy.

What followed was a roller-coaster ride for Rajiv, but entertainment for others. All along the journey, both Sheshan and Aryan deliberately came up with a twisted answer for every trick question of Rajiv. The only dull period was his sleeping time. Otherwise, neither did Rajiv give up, nor Sheshan and Aryan.

They landed at Bamako, the capital of Mali, at 7:00 A.M. local time. The delegation was received by the Minister of Foreign Affairs. Rajiv observed that, albeit, it was an International Airport, there were limited amenities. It was a little more than no frills facility. They were treated as the Country Guests and arrangements were made in a star rated avenue customized to the instructions of Government and capable to comply with the associated protocol. The self-driven escort cars were programmed to move in a set formation, ensuring the safety and fastest route to the venue.

Fraught with apprehensions and prejudice, Rajiv found the hotel to be in stark contrast with his landing impressions. He entered into a royal lobby, ostensibly designed by a seasoned architect. Rooms were embellished with all the modern utilities Rajiv could think of.

He sat on the couch, and tried to infer the state of affairs of the territory he was in, by juxtaposing his 180 degrees apart experiences. Before any conclusion, he was drawn by a knock on the door. It was Aryan carrying the invisible jolt for Rajiv.

"Fresh' n up quickly. We'll have breakfast together and proceed to Timbuktu in a military convoy" – Aryan disclosed the plan.

"At least, you could have said this in the flight" – said Rajiv with friendly anger in his eyes.

"How could we kill entertainment in such a long journey. I'll let you know what's ahead on the breakfast table" – teased Aryan.

Rajiv got ready in time. He was soon at the breakfast table, where he was introduced to **General Seydou Tounkara**, specializing in anti-terrorist and peacekeeping operations. The General was a tall and broad shouldered man, akin to an ancient warlord, born to fight. His strong forearms proudly courted a 3 inch scar and rainbow of medals merrily hung on his uniform. It was an absolute depiction of his abilities and slew the requirement of any verbal or textual representation.

"We shall depart after breakfast. The convoy is ready at the backside" – informed the General in his typical African accent.

"Why rear gate ??" asked Rajiv.

"Security and Secrecy. We are officially here for a trade meet. Moving evidently in a military convoy to a different and sensitive area may raise eyebrows. That's potentially detrimental to our mission and may result in a snowball effect releasing alerts to the enemy" – explained Sheshan.

"But then, what if we are not present in the trade meet. Don't you think we will blow our cover" – asked Rajiv.

"Don't worry. Our names are not in the official list of delegates. So nobody will search for us. We can contentedly concentrate on our mission" – came the disclosure from Aryan.

Finishing the breakfast, three of them followed General Tounkara to the secret exit. Rajiv felt like a VVIP seeing the series of vehicles and their arrangement. At the same time, it signalled a risky and dangerous journey ahead. Tounkara sensed Rajiv's inhibitions and offered the explanation:

"Mali has long been entangled in civil war and extremist attacks. Though, it is subdued as on date, a long journey via highway is still precarious. So, the cavalcade. This is a standard protocol over here for senior officials like me. Travelling with me shall nullify the risk of exposing you people".

Rajiv acknowledged and entered the car earmarked for them. He sat comfortably and observed the terrain.

"This is going to be so unhappening. Seems we won't get to answer any trick questions on this lap" – Aryan broke the silence and nudged Sheshan.

Rajiv knew, he was the target. Now was his turn. He smiled cunningly and rolled back to what he was doing : enjoying the landscape outside. It was a 12 hour ride and they reached their destination around 10:30 in the night. It was the army headquarters in Timbuktu.

Three of them, along with General Seydou Tounkara, then separated from the convoy and changed their vehicle. To their surprise, the co-ordination was so impeccable that without uttering a word, the driver went on to his job. Within 15 minutes their car entered the portico of a cemented building standing in between the ruins of historical architectures destroyed by the stint of extremist captivity.

“Hope this is it. We don’t need to change any further. I am tired and really want to sleep” – whispered Rajiv to Aryan.

“This is just the beginning comrade..” – smiled Aryan

Chapter 11 – The Enemy Network

Not so attractive structure from outside, transformed entirely into a different world by the time Rajiv and Aryan were shown their rooms. A linear expensive carpet ran across the lobby, complementing the aesthetics of granite flooring. Strategic placement of multiple pair of high resolution cameras covered every nook and corner of the lobby and rendered a hawk eye monitoring. Luxurious rooms were comparable to the comfort of any premium resort. The gadgets installed could have been considered as the dream of many tech bravados. Every window had a clandestine spot encapsulating an ultra-modern telescope, allowing the occupant to monitor movements on the streets across the building. There was a special cupboard housing a plethora of sophisticated weapons.

General Tounkara continued to explain the features and rules of the facility:

"This is an X-File Military Installation and the special abilities and equipment present here are privy to a very limited senior army officials. Everything over here is with a purpose. Don't be fooled by the mundane nature. For example, the carpets apart from adding the attractiveness quotient, hide the wires. Walls are also connected to a central command. Any attempt to drill or add a foreign entity, howsoever small, will trigger an alarm somewhere else. In short, I mean to say that if you need anything extra, let me be the first point of contact, basically to avoid any inconveniences".

"Got it" – confirmed Aryan.

"Can I ask a question General" – Rajiv was a little hesitant.

"Of course" – Tounkara was all smiles.

"The self-driving cars of airport were ditched for travel to Timbuktu. I was wondering about it" – elaborated Rajiv.

"Things are different here. The danger of attack looms frequently. Even a slightest technical hitch can lead to loss of the entire battalion. We cannot pre-feed all the possible scenarios to technology. So we prefer to optimize the dependency. Life is more important. Taking manual control of the vehicle allow us to respond to any unplanned and unique situation. The vehicles are fitted with gadgets that are quick to run heuristics and suggest a plan of action, though" – clarified Tounkara.

"Oh, pardon me General. The bottom line is, that the tech worms inside techies, often are the early registrars of minutest alienation of technology" – Rajiv bared his heart.

"It's alright" – replied the General.

"Sheshan was as right as rain in your selection" – complimented Aryan.

While Rajiv accepted it humbly, Sheshan was happy to display a swaggering acceptance of his choice.

"For your information, the enemy is in the building right in front of the east facing window of your rooms. About 800 meters. And yes, we have deliberately allotted adjacent rooms to you all for better co-ordination. Let's disperse now and meet at sharp 8 o'clock tomorrow morning" – intervened General Tounkara.

"As you say General. Thanks a lot for your help" – said Sheshan moving towards his room.

By 8:00 A.M. everyone was at Aryan's room who was sitting next to telescope at his window.

"Looks as if you were working in the night" – came Rajiv's analysis.

Aryan reciprocated with a counter question – "If you are in the network, how long will it take you to do whatever you intend to do ??".

"It would be really nice, if a prior information about their setup is available" – the hacker within Rajiv suddenly shot up.

"Well, that's not up on the platter. Do you have anything without it ??" – frowned Aryan.

"Don't worry, I have a solution to that. If we can push a reconnaissance drone through the enemy's facility, we can get an idea of their set up" – Rajiv played the leg-puller and took out a small chip from his pocket.

"You are talking about this !!" – Aryan was surprised.

"Yes" – was Rajiv's confirmation.

"That can be arranged. We have a local informer, the tea supplier for mafias. He can do the job for us" – winked General Tounkara.

"What if he betrays" – Aryan brought up the possibility.

"Well, then you must know the reason behind our confidence" – said Tounkara and continued:

"We had put this building under surveillance based on the sketch forwarded by Sheshan. We found that the suspect was a regular visitor. The building, is in fact the ruins of community centre destroyed by the extremists. Italian Mafia had cleverly taken it by hiding behind the faces of local businessmen. As on date, it is portrayed as a trading centre for modern gadgets from Europe.

The challenge was to get into the building, without seizing it officially. That's when the tea came to our rescue. Having tea is more like a ritual in Mali, and is traditionally consumed in 3 servings. It's a process in itself and lasts around an hour, often more. The shadow businessmen in the building loved to indulge and treat their esteemed guests on a regular basis. Actually, it marked the point of deal consummation.

Surveillance from our side, led us to this tea supplier, who was their favourite. Knowing our doubts, he readily agreed to help, for his family was wiped out in an extremist attack aided by the mafias. We verified the facts and they were true".

"How early can the drone be deployed" – asked Rajiv.

"Let's see. But it will be done" – assured Tounkara.

By lunch, they received the confirmation of drone being sneaked into the enemy building. Tounkara's aide boasted of slipping it into a room with lots of computers. Rajiv was happy like a child, and instantly unfolded his roll-top which was to act as a remote control.

"Let's have a glimpse of the facility. The drone has got a battery backup of 48 hours" – Rajiv invited others and mirrored his laptop screen to one of the walls designed for the purpose.

Rajiv chuckled and activated the spy drone which slowly transformed into the shape of a miniature dragonfly. Soon it began the constant transmission of its location co-ordinates and recording from the powerful camera mounted on it. Within a few minutes, Rajiv shrieked unexpectedly, as if he had hit the jackpot.

"Whoops !!! we have got into the server room. And what goes in our favour is that the lab is equipped with HT-GTAX-III, the predecessor of HT-GTAX-IV, that we had at our facility. I can get into it in 15 minutes" – announced Rajiv in excitement.

"Ok, then do it" – said Aryan.

"Not that easy buddy. Look at the corner. It's a switch based network. Most probably, they are not connected to the outside world. Considering that, they must be using a different lab for hacking and infecting their targets " – Rajiv defined the problem.

He then followed a security guard to manoeuvre the drone out of the server room. Picture on the wall made Rajiv and others jump from the chairs. It was heavily guarded like a secure military base. Rajiv guided the drone to capture the adjacent locations and slowly reached a room what appeared to be another lab.

"This is it. Look at the routers mounted at the end. This is the lab to infiltrate world networks" – concluded Rajiv.

"Can you accomplish the task from here" – asked Aryan.

"I can take on the hackers lab. But can do nothing about the server room till it is connected to the internet in some form or the other" – replied Rajiv.

"That means, we need to be in the server room to accomplish our mission" – Aryan iterated his comprehension.

"Undoubtedly Yes" – stamped Rajiv

Chapter 12 – The Infection

"Are there cameras installed ??" – enquired Aryan

"I forgot to concentrate on that" – confessed Rajiv.

"Not an issue. Let's do it now" – Aryan took his chair with something clearly running in his mind.

Next 3 hours, Rajiv controlled the movement of drone to scan the corners and ceiling. They could identify quite a few pairs. But Aryan was not satisfied. He requested for several rounds with different starting points. He finally zeroed on a location and asked Rajiv to note down the coordinates of the point.

"That's the safe zone. Cameras might miss it" – said Aryan.

"Do you have a plan ??" – demanded Sheshan.

Aryan nodded and explained the infiltration plan:

"We shall start our mission at 00:30 hrs tonight. I shall be sending conspicuous surveillance drones, both at the front and rear gate of the facility to trigger chaos. Rajiv and I shall utilize this opportunity to teleport ourselves into the server room. Rajiv then finishes the job as quickly as possible. We shall be avoiding any direct contact with the enemy and shall be in the enemy territory for a maximum of 1 hour from teleportation. We shall set the reverse clock and be unerringly back, as soon as the clock shows 00:00. Mission accomplished or mission failed; doesn't matter".

Aryan knew, that the mission was wholly dependent on the teleporting machine installed over there. He looked towards General Tounkara, with his eyes seeking answers in the cult language of a special force.

Formidable soldier as he was, Tounkara displayed a supreme precision in comprehension of question embedded in Aryan's eyes – "Is the machine advanced enough to be relied on for the mission ??"

"Not a problem. The machine is capable of teleporting upto 2000 meters. We are merely 800-900 meters away. Also, it can be held for 2.5 hours, once activated. It's a perfect fit to your plan" – came a confident assurance from Tounkara.

"Ahh. I need only 15 minutes. We'll be back in a flash" – Said Rajiv.

"If everything goes as planned" – giggled Aryan while scaring the hell out of Rajiv.

Aryan then went on to set the machines and check the weapons he would carry on the mission. Sheshan, on the other hand, moved with General Tounkara for discussion. Rajiv was left alone.

"What am I supposed to do ??" – complained Rajiv.

"Go and prepare yourself" – replied Aryan with a shrug.

Rajiv put up a brave face and went to his room. Aryan was ready for the show by 00:20 hrs. So was Rajiv. Now it was Aryan's turn. He synchronized Rajiv's watch with that of his, and handed him a remote.

"Press the centre button in case of danger. It will immediately teleport you back" – explained Aryan

Exactly at 00:30 hrs, he released the drones. 2 at front and 2 at rear. As expected, there was chaos on the enemy side. Havoc was created by Aryan's last minute improvisation. He sent 2 more drones on left and right flank. The plan was working, and on the first opportunity, Rajiv and Aryan teleported into the server room.

"Beautiful !!!" – was the spontaneous response of Rajiv on seeing the set up.

He immediately received a blow on his back from Aryan.

"We are not on a sight seeing trip. We are in a hostile territory. Just finish your job fast and move out from here, you fool !!!" – he whispered.

Rajiv quickly connected his roll-top and fixed a static image to dodge the security cameras. He then moved to the server in a blitz. Rajiv swiftly initiated the process of uploading bugs in the server and simultaneously cloning the storage.

"How long ??" – asked Aryan.

"20 minutes" – replied Rajiv

"Extra 5 minutes !!!" – Aryan exclaimed with a deep stare.

"It's still less than an hour. Now don't disturb and let me do my job. Or else, it may extend beyond 20 minutes" – warned Rajiv.

Aryan, being a soldier, knew the risk of a single extra minute inside the enemy boundary. He let Rajiv do his job, but displayed a rapid metamorphism to a vigilante on a high alert. He had to be predominantly observant, to provide the protective cover to Rajiv. Everything was fine, up until the climax.

Rajiv was almost done, when he and Aryan were spotted by a security guard who swiftly locked the room and raised the alarm. Rajiv immediately pushed the button on his remote to be teleported back to the hotel room, but failed miserably.

"You can't be teleported if you are one meter away from the teleporting co-ordinates" – informed Aryan.

"You never said this before" – Rajiv was visibly petrified.

Entire past communication lost its significance when they heard a daunting voice from the loudspeaker installed in the room.

"You are on our radar. If you attempt anything silly, you will be served a poisonous gas which you may not like. You have 5 minutes . Make up your mind – either co-operate with us or WELCOME TO HELL..."

"If I die, it will be because of you" – said Rajiv in a trembling voice.

"If you die, you are dead. That's it. No further analysis stupid. Now shut up and let me think" – scolded Aryan.

He slowly took Rajiv to the teleporting co-ordinates, and pressed the button on remote which outrightly refused to come in action. It was a surprise, because Rajiv had already disabled the jammers.

"I think we are enclosed within thick steel doors. May be, it has led to the weakening of teleporting signals" – surmised Aryan looking carefully at the steel gates.

"Is your work done ??" – he asked Rajiv.

"Yes, I have got the clone and bugged the network here. Other lab doesn't need any special treatment. I entered their system through my roll-top, even before coming here. I think within 5 minutes there will be a surge in internal voltage of the systems, thereby, permanently damaging the drives and circuits. But it can be detected only after a few minutes, when fumes start coming out of the digital boxes" – briefed Rajiv.

"Very good, and We have 5 minutes. Mission Successful !!!. Now listen carefully. Stay here and be inactive. As soon as the door opens, we press the button of the remote on the count of 3" – Aryan looked at Rajiv who nodded in agreement.

What Aryan didn't tell, was that he was entirely banking on his theory of steel gates. He awfully hoped it to work against all odds. By the time Aryan was praying, the two were double crossed by the enemy. The doors opened before 5 minutes, setting loose an army of sophisticated brutes, ready to rush, detain and celebrate the capture of their prey.

Aryan looked at Rajiv, who was quick to take the cue and synchronize himself with Aryan's counting fingers. They pressed the remote button on the count of 3 and within seconds were back in Aryan's room.

Next 5 minutes, Rajiv couldn't regain his sane self. "Thank God" – was all he could utter while lying on the couch.

"Great Job" – complimented Aryan

"You underestimated me.." – Rajiv was out of breath and strove to hide his fright under a wicked smile.

"But what about your bugs. Did they really work ?? We came out before the effects" – recalled Aryan

"Let's find out" – the confidence in Rajiv's voice was no abatement of confusion on Aryan's face

Chapter 13 – The Destruction

"Come, have a look. Before teleporting, I released 2 miniature drones. Let's see, what's going on there. Welcome to a brand new episode!!" – Rajiv rode on to his thespian self, connected to the drones and projected his roll-top on the wall.

The server room of Italian mafia was in a mess. The bug was successful and the systems were emitting smoke in series. Frustration was pervasive in the evil spirits moving in the room. Rajiv switched over to the drone in the lab. There too, Rajiv's worms did their job in the most efficient manner. The result was nothing less than spectacular for Rajiv and Aryan.

"Hurray. My virus is working. Now any system over there which is connected to the network will be destroyed" – happiness glared in Rajiv.

"Impressive" – true praise came from Aryan.

Engrossed in the success of the mission, Rajiv and Aryan experienced a kind of volcanic eruption when decibels of speakers in the room surged exponentially. General Tounkara along with his battalion had raided the Italian mafia base.

"What's this ??" – Rajiv could not hold back.

"It's as per the plan" – Aryan was not moved.

"When was this decided ??" – Rajiv was curious.

"You didn't pay attention to my narrative. Remember, I told everbody - ***Mission accomplished or mission failed; doesn't matter***. That was the clue. Either attack would be immediately on our return, or after 1 hour from our teleporting" – detailed Aryan.

"What if we were captured ??" – asked Rajiv.

"Soldiers are trained for such situations. In that case, I would have tried to mislead the enemy, till the arrival of reinforcement" – Aryan continued with his revelations.

"What if we were killed ??" – Rajiv's imagination had no boundaries.

"That's collateral damage in military parlance" – Aryan was enjoying Rajiv's perspiration.

"No. It's inhuman" – complained Rajiv.

"So is WAR !!! " – Aryan was relentless.

The conversation shuddered Rajiv from within. He got a glimpse of situation Aryan and other soldiers find themselves in on a regular basis. He felt fortunate to have returned alive.

"Look, General is done. They have taken over" – cheered Aryan while staring at the wall.

"Yups, I'am going to sleep now" – Rajiv was extremely tired.

He slept till lunch.

"How are you" – Sheshan inquired as Rajiv joined for the feast.

"Good" – replied Rajiv with a smile.

Post lunch, they met General Tounkara to express their gratitude.

"Had it not been you General, we would have surely failed. Thanks a lot" – said Sheshan.

"My pleasure gentlemen. It was beneficial for us too. We were totally unaware about an enemy base so close to us. I owe it to you" – reciprocated Tounkara.

Convoy for their return was ready. They left at 2:00 and reached Bamako at midnight. That night, Rajiv had a deep sleep, free of worries. Next morning, there was an official ceremony, bestowing bravery accolade of Mali to three heroes – ***General Seydou Tounkara, Aryan and Rajiv.***

Within few hours of valedictory session attached to the award ceremony; Sheshan, Rajiv and Aryan were flying back to India along with other delegates.

"Have you studied the clone you brought from the server room" – Sheshan asked Rajiv mid-air.

"Yes. Your facility was the fourth" – Rajiv's findings were little more than Sheshan had thought.

"Could you please explain" – Sheshan didn't understand much.

Rajiv elaborated:

"They had attacked government systems across the country and accumulated data from 3 sources. ***Number one, Ministry;*** *they had access to the initial draft of the concept report. I think, that's the source of rumours regarding our special weapon program.* ***Number two, Project Phase 1, Beta; facility of the team giving inputs to my office.*** *Apparently, they eyed the walk-through model. But could lay hands only on the section detailing with the list of software under consideration.* ***Number 3, Phase 2(a); from my office.*** *They stole a portion of theoretical paper developed by us. However, it's of no use without the Software Requirement Specification (SRS).*

Next was your office. Obviously they didn't get any information from Shah. Also, they had developed 2 lists. One of the governments interested in prototype and another that of powerful entities who could grace the illegal weapon market and participate in the auction".

"Gosh !! Shah was our prize catch" – Sheshan's sigh was palpable.

"I didn't get it" – Rajiv switched to anxious mode.

"Shah was due to contact enemy after a few days. We nabbed him, but did not lay our hands on the mafia agent. So, they never knew we were after them. And all this while, Sriram was kept in the loop. The moment General Tounkara initiated the assault, he was cleared to arrest the mafia agent" – said Sheshan preparing for a nap.

It was another shocker for Rajiv. "Man, I feel like retiring" – he was drained of breaking news hitting him at regular intervals.

"This is just the beginning" - Aryan laughed his heart out.

Rajiv could hardly make out anything from Aryan's statement.

"What does that mean. Beginning !!. The mission is already over. Now what ??" he said to himself.

Answers were surely not be found there. Rajiv could only wait to reach back home, how so restless the feeling be.

Chapter 14 – Homecoming

After two days, the three of them reached the special facility where they received a well-planned and grand welcome. Everybody shouted 3 cheers for Rajiv. They were then taken to a table decorated with champagne, sumptuous dishes and exotic desserts. Milieu was drenched in the feeling of farewell, readily cherished by one and all, who were the guests of special facility for past 19 days.

After the celebrations, Sheshan thanked the entire team for support and dedication to the National cause. He informed that there will be a strongly scripted press conference, next afternoon, to end the abduction drama. Everybody can then return to their normal life.

"There is only one instruction. You should never discuss this with anybody ever. At least for many years from now. Remember, it's for your safety and national interest" – Sheshan laid the rules.

Everyone dispersed for preparation of homecoming. Sheshan then went to Rajiv and broke the news that he had been chosen to head the cyber security division. He also disclosed that on his return, Rajiv was supposed to report to a location as mentioned in the letter which he shall receive after the press conference.

"You must devise a better network. We are banking on you. I wanted it to be a surprise for you, but could not hold any longer" – said Sheshan with a pleasant helplessness.

"Do you want something more ??" – Sheshan gave the option.

"A little break before taking up the new assignment" – said Rajiv with a grin.

"Granted" – came the immediate reply from Sheshan.

Rajiv set out for his home after the scheduled press conference. He was received by teary eyed Saumya who could barely speak. She just clung on to Rajiv, held him tight and said – "Don't do this again. Can't you change your job".

"As you wish, madam" – said Rajiv showing the letter of new location and profile.

"See, we think so alike. That's true love. You did it even before I said" – Saumya was blushing.

Rajiv could sense an innocent satisfaction on Saumya's face. She actually believed that he had shifted his job that led to his abduction and he is safe now. Rajiv was emotionally hypnotized by such a simple thought process; selfless love.

He said to himself:

"I nearly died. But even if I want, I can't share my true story for security reasons. Things are uncertain. But I must ascertain one opportunity. I have few days before I join. I am gonna live it to the fullest. It's time to surprise my family with an impromptu holiday plan. My 100% of the time shall be for Saumya and family members. Sneha must get her story. Maybe, she could tell her own or pass on this one, someday in the future; Near or distant far, whatever the fate decides"

Rajiv entered his home thinking of innovative and enchanting ways to put up the surprise. What followed him was one iron resolve :

"There must be at least one such vacation every year. You never know which one will make a story, to hold on forever".